MW00929856

Pillow Talk

...and other tales

a collection of
short stories by
Marisa Bonilla

©2022 Marisa Bonilla

All Rights Reserved.
Cover art and layout by Tony De Luz

MARIANDA PRESS
SEDONA · ARIZONA
www.mariandapress.com

Dedication

To my daughter Rennie

Also by Marisa Bonilla

Hotel Summer
A simpler, more innocent time, a time of long car trips, comic books, lemon cookies and old-time movie stars

Spain Revisited
Follow along on a newly-divorced woman's journey to self-discovery in 1965 Spain.

Pillow Talk and Other Tales

Table of Contents

Pillow Talk

"You are such a good husband. Have I told you lately how much I love you?"

"Your body language is telling me now. Your head is resting on my shoulder, your left leg is on my thighs, and your arms are gently embracing my chest."

"I just love snuggling up to your warm naked body!"

"And I love holding you and stroking your head. Your hair feels like silk and smells like a bouquet of roses."

"It must be the shampoo I'm using."

"No. It's because, to me, you are a beautiful red rose in full bloom, open and trusting. You delight all of my senses."

"Flattery will get you everywhere."

"Will you marry me?"

"I thought you'd never ask."

"You always say that."

"It's because I want you to ask me again."

"All right. This time, 'yes' or 'no'. Will you marry me?"

"Yes!"

"After all these years, are you still glad you married me?"

"Let's say, I wouldn't trade you for Antonio Banderas."

"Well, I'm no movie star, but I'm faithful."

"And you don't smoke, and you have a wonderful, mischievous sense of humor. You laugh so spontaneously. I like that. Actually, you have opened me up to being able to laugh out loud."

"I'm glad. When we first started dating, you would just smile at my jokes. Now, you actually join in with a ladylike laugh."

"Well, you do say some funny things at times. I can't help but laugh, ladylike or not."

"I love to hear you laugh. It means I have succeeded in opening you up a little."

"You have, in more ways than you know. I am so grateful to have you in my life."

"I feel the same way."

"It's so wonderful to be able to snuggle up and fall asleep with your arms hugging me. I feel so comforted and secure in your love, no matter what kind of day I've had."

"Ditto, Sweetheart."

"It's so wonderful that we still like to do things together."

"Yes, like cooking together. You make the main dish. I make the salad."

"And we share in the cleanup. We're a team!"

"I'm the luckiest man in town. I bet that not many wives greet their husbands with a kiss and a hot cup of freshly brewed coffee every morning."

"I love to please you."

"You do, and always have. Things have changed since we were younger, but not our shared enjoyment of doing things together. Remember when we first got married how on the weekends we'd ride our bicycles through the wealthy neighborhoods and admire the beautifully kept gardens? Then, we'd come home with ideas for our own garden?"

"Yes, I do. I especially focused on the rose gardens. I liked how they were planted. When they bloomed, they resembled a beautiful bouquet of different colored roses. Then, we came home and planted our own rose garden. I arranged the plants according to color so we'd have our own rose bouquet to enjoy."

"And I planted them for you. Well, we still garden together, but there isn't much to do now that we live in a condominium."

"True, but we still plant flowers in pots."

"Condominiums have their pros and cons, Sweetheart, but we're closer to the fire department and the police station. If we have a problem, they could respond within five to ten minutes."

"*If* we call them, Honey. Remember the night we had just fallen asleep when we were suddenly awakened by two men standing at the foot of our bed shining their high-powered flashlights right at our heads?"

"Yes, I do. I couldn't see them very well because it was dark, and I was half blinded by their flashlights. But from what I could see, they were dressed alike in dark clothing and wore black baseball caps."

"You were so brave. You sat up in bed so quickly that the sheet dropped down to barely cover your private parts. They could easily see that you were naked. Then, you said, 'Hi ya fellas.'"

"That was a stupid thing for me to say."

"Well, you did surprise them. You could have asked, 'How can I help you?' Our burglars, or whoever they were, were

3

so shocked to see two white-haired octogenarians, stark naked from the waist up, that they turned and, without saying a word, left as abruptly as they had come. When I was sure that they were gone, I had to get up to see if the front door was locked. It wasn't!"

"When you came back to bed, you were shivering and so cold. I told you to snuggle up and I'd get you warm."

"But, why were they here? And why did they leave so abruptly without saying a word?"

"I don't know, Sweetheart. I haven't the slightest clue. We certainly didn't call the fire department or the police. I think that, whoever they were, they might have had keys, or maybe I just didn't lock the front door. I do have a tendency to forget things. The main thing is that they came and went, and we were not harmed in any way."

"I'm sure that God sent His angels to protect us."

"It's time for sleep, Sweetheart."

"One last kiss?"

"One last kiss."

"Sleep well, Sweetheart."

"Sleep well, my dearest love."

Ladies' Lunch

I had just turned fifty. Several of my best friends were married to men in my husband's law firm. I wanted to invite them to help me celebrate my birthday at a ladies' lunch. As one of my birthday presents, my husband offered to pay the bill. I chose the old, prestigious Pasadena Huntington Hotel. I called my friends. Joan said she could come, as did Trisha and Suzanne. Helen had an appointment that day she could not change.

When I called the hotel to make a reservation, I asked for a quiet corner table. There was bound to be lively conversation as we liked to catch up on what had happened to each of us since we last had lunch together.

Joan arrived first. We hugged.

"I'm so glad you could come, Joan."

"I wouldn't have missed it. I love our 'catch-up' get-togethers."

Then Tricia and Suzanne arrived.

"Thank you for coming, ladies!"

"And thank you for choosing the Huntington Hotel for our luncheon, Ann. It's such a charming Old-World hotel."

"You're welcome, Suzanne."

"By the way, happy birthday, Ann. It's a big one I believe."

"Yes, Trisha, number fifty."

"I'm next. My birthday is in June. I don't know where it will be yet, but I'm inviting all of you to my birthday luncheon now."

"Well, ladies, since we are all assembled, shall we go into the dining room? I requested a corner table in a quiet spot."

When we were all seated, our waiter came to our table and asked, "May I bring you ladies something to drink besides water?"

I looked at the wine list and said, "I'd like a glass of your Sonoma chardonnay."

"Excellent choice." He turned to Joan and asked. "And you, madam?"

"I'll have your house pinot grigio. It's always good."

The waiter then turned to Trisha. "I'll have the same."

"And you, madam?" he asked Suzanne. "I'll have the Sonoma chardonnay."

When the waiter returned with our drink orders he also brought the luncheon menus.

"Are you ready to order now, ladies, or shall I give you a minute to decide and come back later?"

I looked briefly at the menu and ordered fish and chips. Joan told the waiter she would have the same.

Trisha said, "I'm on a diet so I'll just have a Caesar salad. Oh, I see it can come with shrimp or chicken. I'll have it with the shrimp."

"Excellent choice, madam." Next was Suzanne. "And you, madam?"

"I'd like your club sandwich. I've had it here before, and it's really the best I've had anywhere."

"Thank you, madam. Our club sandwich is our most popular luncheon plate."

When the waiter had taken our orders he bowed, thanked us, and left.

After he returned with our wine and had served everyone, I raised my glass and said, "To friendship and to the many years that we have been friends."

Then, Joan raised her glass and said, "To birthdays!"

Tricia was next. "To 'catch-ups'!"

Suzanne lifted her glass with the final toast. "To many more!"

I turned to my left and said, "Let's start our 'catch-ups' with you, Joan."

Joan picked up her purse and pulled out some photos. "You know me, I just can't resist bringing photos of my grandchildren. Since we last met, Bill and I have been blessed with two new grandbabies. John and his wife, Alice, had another girl, and Bob and his wife, Katherine, had another boy." As she passed the photos to Trisha, she pointed to the one of a baby wrapped in a pink blanket and said, "This is Amy. She is three months old now." Then, Joan pointed to the second photo and said, "This is Elizabeth, Amy's big sister."

Trisha asked, "How old is she now?"

"She's three."

Trisha looked at the photos for a long moment before she said, "They are absolutely adorable!" Then, she passed them on to Suzanne who was equally enthusiastic in her comments about Joan's grandchildren.

When the photos came to me, I looked at each one again and again before I said, "You are indeed blessed, Joan. You have beautiful grandchildren." As I handed them back to Joan I thought, "I wish they were mine." Ed and I were childless.

As Joan put the photos back in her purse I asked her, "Tell us about your daughter, Marilyn. I know that she got engaged to Dan Roberts. Has she set a date for the wedding yet?"

"I hate to tell you, but the big wedding my daughter was planning is off."

"What happened, Joan?"

"If Marilyn finds out that I told you what *really* happened, she would be furious that I shared her secret with friends."

"Don't worry, Joan. When we play 'catch up,' whatever comes up, never leaves the room. Right, ladies?"

They all nodded their heads in agreement and each said, "Correct!"

"Well, as I said, the wedding is off. Dan gave Marilyn an engagement gift she didn't like, and she gave him back his engagement ring."

"Why?" I asked.

"This is hard to say. Dan gave our daughter a sexually transmitted disease."

"Oh, Joan, how awful! Thank God Marilyn didn't marry him. What a cheating rat!"

"Thank you, Trisha. Of course, Marilyn was devastated. She really loved Dan and was hoping to start a family as soon as they got married. I don't think she'll ever be able to get over what he did to her."

"Oh, I'm so sorry that this happened to Marilyn. The last time we got together you told us how happy she was and how excited about having a big church wedding."

"Thanks, Suzanne. What's done is done. Bill didn't really like Dan. He said that Dan was a show-off and talked only about himself."

"How is she taking their breakup?" I asked.

"Not well. I'm so worried about her. She is obviously depressed. She hardly eats a thing. I know that she isn't sleeping well. I tried to get her to talk about what happened, but all she says is, 'I don't want to talk about it.' "

"I'm sorry, Joan, that you and your husband have to deal with this problem too."

"Thank you, Trisha. I guess all we can do is reassure Marilyn that we love her and that we'll get through this heartbreak together."

"Well," said Tricia, "I'm next in line for 'catch-up,' so I may as well come out with my story. My husband didn't give me a sexually transmitted disease, but he cheated on me with a girl young enough to be his daughter."

"Oh, Trisha, I'm so sorry. I thought that you and Charlie had an ideal marriage!"

"So did I, Ann, but that's not all the news. Charlie had been having an affair with this girl for several months, and she got pregnant. He told me what had happened and said that he wanted a divorce so he could marry his girlfriend."

"Are you going to divorce him?" asked Suzanne.

"Yes."

"I hope you take him to the cleaners!"

"I hope to do just that, Suzanne. Upon the recommendation of a friend who got a divorce last year, I hired her lawyer. He is well-known as a Beverly Hills divorce lawyer who gets everything his client wants and more."

"I hope Charlie gets what's coming to him. You were a

good and faithful wife. I hope your lawyer leaves your cheating husband penniless!"

"Thanks, Suzanne. Well, to start, I'll get the house—mortgage free. Once Charlie moves out all his clothes and his possessions, I'm going to redecorate the house, starting with my bedroom. The king-size bed will be replaced with a queen. I look forward to buying a new bedspread, sheets, blankets, even pillows. I always hated those oversized king pillows Charlie wanted."

"Good for you, Trisha. I hope you redecorate your entire house."

"Maybe. First comes my bedroom. Then me. I want to get back to my previous size ten and then buy a whole new up-to-date wardrobe. But before that happens, I'm thinking of going to a health and wellness spa in Arizona where my friend Barbara went after her divorce. She came back looking fabulous."

"Good for you, Trisha! You are a strong woman. You'll get through this difficult time and be okay. We all love you and will support you any way we can. I think you're on the right path. Redoing your bedroom is the first step."

"Thanks, Joan."

"And I like the idea of your going to a health spa. Is it terribly expensive?"

"I'll find out, Ann. I sent for the spa's brochure. My friend Barbara stayed two weeks and took advantage of all the spa's activities and treatments, but didn't tell me what it cost. I'll share what I find out with you, if you'd like."

"Oh, yes, please."

"Trisha, it's good that you'll be distracted with your plans for getting on with your life, but honestly, how do you feel about what Charlie did to you?"

"How do I *feel?*"

"Yes, be honest."

"Ann, I feel hurt, abandoned, sometimes extremely angry, and want my revenge. Then, sometimes, I get very depressed and miss Charlie and our life together before he left me for a younger woman. I guess I still love him."

"I'm sure my daughter has similar feelings, but she won't talk about them. It's good that you can share how your feel with us and know that what you say is our secret and won't be talked about elsewhere."

"Thank you, Joan. I very much appreciate that you all are there for me. I feel very blessed. Enough about me and my coming divorce. You're next, Suzanne."

"Well, I'm pleased to say that Tom and I are happily married, and Tommy and Suzie are now in college. Suzie is engaged to be married, and we are starting to plan her wedding, which will be soon after she graduates."

"Congratulations, Suzanne."

"Believe me, Joan, I could have had another story to tell. I came close to getting a divorce when Tommy was six and Suzie, four. I had been suspicious for some time why my husband wasn't home for dinner most nights. He said that he needed to unwind and work out at the Athletic Club after office hours, and that he would eat dinner there. Well, it turns out that several nights a week he was getting his exercise and dinner, not at the Club, but at his 'office wife's' apartment. You know, I'm sure, that office wife is what the lawyers in the law firm call their secretaries. I knew that something fishy was going on, especially when Tom came home smelling like a brewery and went right to bed, saying that he had had a long day and was tired."

11

"What did you do?"

"I hired a detective to follow Tom after he left the office. The detective followed Tom for a week and confirmed my suspicions that something fishy was indeed going on. He photographed Tom entering his secretary's building several times a week and leaving two to three hours later. The other nights the detective photographed Tom at the Athletic Club working out and having dinner there. So, part of Tom's story was true."

"Suzanne, you are a really smart woman. Not many women would have thought to do what you did. Did you confront Tom with the photos?"

"Yes, but before I did, I asked Mom to take the children to her house for the weekend. I didn't want them present when I confronted Tom with the evidence of his cheating on me. He admitted that he had been having an 'after hours' affair with his secretary for several months and asked if I wanted a divorce."

"What else could you possibly do under the circumstances?"

"Ann, I loved Tom. I didn't want to lose him and, besides, the children needed a father *at home.* So, I gave him an ultimatum: You will come home as soon as the office closes. You will be here *before* dinner, spend time with the children, and eat dinner with your family. On weekends, you will go to Tommy's Little League baseball practice and games, and go to church with the family on Sundays. Otherwise, I will divorce you. If I do, you will face huge child support and spousal payments, mortgage payments, and whatever else a divorce lawyer can get that will leave you penniless each month for many years. Then, there will be college expenses for the children; so expect that you will have to contribute to their college funds each and every month."

"What did he say, Suzanne?"

"He said, 'I'll do it.' Then, I said, another thing. "You will fire your secretary!" He came back with, "But, Suzanne, I can't. I've had her for a long time. She's indispensable."

"You can get another one, or use the office pool."

"Well, Tom wasn't happy with that last requirement, but after much protesting he finally agreed to all the terms."

"What happened next?"

"Well, Ann, I cooked his favorite meal for his first dinner home with the family. I wore his favorite color, blue. I tried really hard to be as positive as I possibly could, considering that I was still very angry with Tom. I assume that he was angry with me, too."

"How did you resolve your anger with one another?"

"The children helped. Tom is a good father and loves his children. He got the idea to build a swimming pool in our backyard, which was mostly lawn anyway. After work and on the weekends, he spent a lot of time in the pool with the children. He taught them how to swim."

"What about *you*, Suzanne. And your relationship with Tom?"

"Well, we had what you might call a 'second honeymoon.' Mom came over to babysit the children for a weekend, and Tom and I went to San Francisco. We stayed at the Mark Hopkins Hotel, went to the zoo, and had some great seafood at the wharf. We talked a lot, and Tom asked me to forgive him for cheating on me with his secretary. He said that he still loved me and wanted his family back."

"Did you forgive him?"

"Yes, of course. I never stopped loving Tom. I wanted

13

him back."

"No more rocks in the mattress?"

"No more rocks in the mattress, Joan."

"I'm glad. I like happy endings!"

"Ann, I believe it's your turn to play 'catch up.' "

"Well, ladies, I'm grateful that I can tell you that Ed and I have a very happy marriage. I don't believe that any of you know that I was married before I met Ed. Frankly, it was a very painful marriage that I preferred to keep secret, even from Ed."

"Secrets can make you sick, Ann. It's good that you can share it with us. You know that we will never disclose any personal information we hear."

"Thank you, Joan. I guess I might as well come out with it. As I said, I was married before I met Ed. It was to Peter, a college friend who I met in my English class. He was brilliant and movie-star handsome. I was crazy about him. When he asked me to marry him, I was quick to say yes, even though I really knew nothing about his past or his family background. We had been married only a few weeks when I found out that he was cheating on me with a mutual college friend."

"Did you confront him?"

"Yes. You probably assume that it was with another woman, but my secret is that Peter was cheating on me with another man."

"How awful! Did you divorce him?"

"Yes, Trisha. There was no way I could go on with the marriage and continue to live with the fear of Peter continuing to cheat on me, and perhaps infecting me with a sexually transmitted disease or even AIDS."

"Were you ever able to forgive him for marrying you to hide his homosexuality?"

"Eventually, yes, but not for a very long time. By sharing my secret with dear friends I feel that I am now even more able to let go of the past."

"The past is past, Ann."

"Yes, Suzanne, the past *is* past. I feel so relieved that I could open up and share my secret with you, my special friends. I guess that is what Ladies' Lunch and 'catch up' is all about. Now, before we go our separate ways, I'd like us to raise our empty glasses to a toast to the women who loved and lost their men. 'May they find new love and happiness.' "

The Neighbors
Part One

"I'm so glad that you came to spend your college spring break with us, Dear. It's been a while since we've had a visit. Grandpa Jim and I so enjoy our time with you."

"I'm glad I could come, Grandma. I'll have to do some reading for my English Lit class, but I'll still have time for a cooking lesson with you. I want to learn how you make all of Grandpa Jim's favorite dishes. Soon, I'll have a recipe box full of your recipes and can look forward to cooking for my future husband. I remember you saying more than once, 'The way to a man's heart is through his stomach.' "

"Yes, Laura. It's an old saying, but I still like to think it's true. Now, how about a nice cup of tea? I just bought some fruit flavored herbal teas. I've already tried the raspberry one, which I think you'd like."

"You know how much I love raspberries, Grandma. Thank you. Are any of Grandpa Jim's raspberry bushes producing yet?"

"Yes. We had some raspberries for breakfast a few mornings ago. I'm assuming there should be enough ripe ones for you to pick for tomorrow's breakfast. I remember when you were little, how you enjoyed picking them."

"Yes. When I did that, I always ate more right off the bush than I picked for breakfast. When raspberries were scarce, I loved hunting for the ripe ones. It was like hunting for the eggs the Easter Bunny left Easter morning."

"I remember watching you, Dear. It was such fun for me,

too, to see you having fun."

"Grandma, I see that the Olsen house is up for sale. What happened?"

"Well, when Mr. Olsen died, Olga had a very hard time adjusting to being a widow. She was very depressed and hardly ever left her house except to buy a few groceries. She and John were very close. They did everything together, especially after he retired. They liked the same things. They were talking about taking a trip to Sweden to visit family when he died rather suddenly of a heart attack."

"Oh, I'm so sorry to hear that, Grandma. I really liked Mrs. Olsen. She was always so nice to me. Remember when we went to her house for tea and her delicious cookies and I admired her new chicken clock? When the alarm went off, it cried 'cock a doodle doo.' She called the clock 'Charlie Chicken.' When I returned home, there was a package from her. Guess what was in it? 'Charlie Chicken'!"

"Yes, I remember her telling me that she wanted you to have it since you were so delighted with the rooster alarm clock."

"I was! I still love waking up to its 'cock a doodle doo.' "

"Olga was a very wonderful neighbor. We miss her, and John, too. When she decided to sell her house and move to be with her daughter in Palo Alto, we knew that it was the best decision for her. It's close to Stanford University, and she will enjoy the cultural activities there. Plus, it's close to San Francisco. She will enjoy shopping at the department stores and all the attractions and amenities that the city offers. Olga and John used to love spending long weekends together going to plays and musical events and eating out at one of the seafood restaurants on the wharf."

"When I was about your age, my grandparents took me to San Francisco for the weekend. While my grandfather attended to some business, my grandmother and I went to the zoo. Then, my grandfather treated us to an amazing dinner at his favorite Chinese restaurant. The next day, my grandmother took me to her favorite department store called 'The City of Paris' and bought me a navy blue coat and a couple of dresses."

"You have a good memory, Grandma!"

"Well, for some things, but if I leave my list at home when I go grocery shopping, I'm in trouble. Olga used to complain that she did that, too. We were so worried about her after John died. She became more and more forgetful about losing things like her car keys. She even forgot to pay her bills. She seemed more and more depressed. We were relieved when her daughter persuaded her to sell her house and move in with her."

"Mrs. Olson was lucky to have you and Grandpa Jim to look after her when Mr. Olson died."

"Did I hear someone mention my name? After I wash up from working in the garden, may I join you ladies for tea?"

"We're having raspberry-flavored tea, Jim. Would you like to try some?"

"No, thank you. I'd rather have my usual tea—just plain black tea."

"We were just talking about our neighbor, Olga Olsen."

"Well, I'm sure that it was all good talk. She was such a good neighbor, not like our neighbor lady next door, Edna Johnson."

"Well, Jim, I wasn't going to talk about Edna Johnson. It could be considered gossip, and it's not nice to talk about people's negative behavior."

"Well, if it's about the person in question, I think it's okay if you keep it confidential. You know that George Johnson and I talk over our shared fence quite often. He usually wants to talk about what's bothering him. Over the years, he's confided more and more about his problems with his wife."

"Well, you know, Jim, she comes over unannounced at our back door about ten in the morning at least once a week just to complain about her husband."

"And Grandma, when I was here on my last visit she mostly came over to complain about her husband's snoring and how he keeps her awake most of the night."

"I told her that Grandpa and I have to take our hearing aids out at night so we don't hear each other snore. I thought she would at least get a smile out of my comment, but she didn't."

"Why doesn't she divorce Mr. Johnson if she's not happy with him?"

"I don't think that snoring is grounds for a divorce. Do you, Jim?"

"Well, as my mother used to say, 'When a marriage goes on the rocks, the rocks are generally in the mattress.' Her husband's not happy either. This morning, he told me that Edna burned the toast again, and that last night she served him overcooked broccoli, knowing he hates broccoli and can't stand looking at it, especially when it's overcooked. I asked him if he knew why she seemed so nasty. 'Well, Jim,' he said, 'she's mad at me because she told me that she wanted diamond earrings for her birthday, and I told her that I just couldn't afford them right now. I'm sure that is why she's giving me such a hard time. I made a mistake marrying a woman so much younger than me. We just aren't on the same page about most things.' Then I asked him, "How much younger than you is she, George?"

"Twenty years, Jim. After my wife Alice died, I was too quick to marry again. Alice and I didn't have any children, and I thought that I would have a second chance at being a father, but Edna didn't want children. She wanted to travel, take cruises, and see the world. And spend as much money as she could. Money has been a problem from the beginning of our marriage."

All I could say was, "I'm sorry, George."

"Well, Jim," he said, "I've made my marriage vows, and I'll keep them. When I die, Edna will get all of my money, and she can do what she wants with it."

"Then George changed the subject. I could see that he didn't want to discuss his marital problems anymore. So he said, 'By the way, Jim, how are the berries doing? I so enjoyed the boysenberries you gave me yesterday.' I told him I'd have some more to give him in a couple of days. 'Thanks for listening,' he said, waved, and left."

"Poor Mr. Johnson. I feel sorry for him, Grandpa."

"I feel sorry for both of them, Laura. It's obvious their marriage is on the rocks."

Part Two
A Year Later

"It's so good I could come again during my spring break, Grandma. I graduate in June, and I think I'll be going to graduate school on the East Coast. I haven't decided where I'll go yet, but I've been accepted at several universities."

"We're so proud of you, Dear. Grandpa and I will definitely be at your graduation and see you get your bachelor's degree. Hopefully, we will also be at your graduation from whichever university you decide to attend to get your master's degree."

"I have a long road ahead, Grandma, before that happens."

"I'm sure it will pass quickly and that you will then find the job that you have worked so hard to prepare for."

"Well, as you know, I want to work with children at the kindergarten and primary level. So, I'll need not only a teaching credential, but also a specialization in music education."

"Keep your goal always in sight, Dear. Be positive. One step at a time, as Grandpa Jim would say."

"Did I hear my name mentioned?"

"Oh, Jim, we were just about to have a mid-morning cup of tea."

"That sounds tempting. May I join you lovely ladies?"

"Yes, of course, Jim. I saw that you were talking to our new neighbor, Charlie Richardson, this morning. Anything new?"

22

"No, not really. Charlie wants to plant some roses for his wife, Betty, and wanted my advice."

"Grandpa Jim, when I first arrived I noticed that the 'For Sale' sign was gone and wondered what kind of new neighbors bought the Olsen house."

"Well, so far they seem friendly enough."

"Jim, I was about to fill Laura in about the neighbors. So much has happened since she was here last year."

"Go ahead, Martha."

"First, the Olsen house was bought by Charlie and Betty Richardson. They are a retired couple who seem to like to travel and are gone a lot of the time. We really haven't had a chance to get to know them very well yet."

"And what about George and Edna Johnson, Grandma?"

"Well, soon after you left, Edna was killed in a car accident coming home from a luncheon in Monterey with an old high school friend. They planned to go to the Monterey Bay Aquarium first, then have lunch in Cannery Row. Edna loved seafood. A favorite restaurant of hers there serves a great crab cocktail and a calamari dish she especially liked. According to her friend, and the police report, she also had two or maybe three margaritas during their two hour lunch. Anyway, Edna's blood alcohol level was beyond the legal limit. I think the police report said that it was 0.10%. The legal limit is 0.08%.

"It was raining pretty heavily when Edna left Monterey. According to the police report, she was driving behind a slow-moving car, got impatient, and started to pass. She apparently didn't see the oncoming car. She sped up to avoid hitting the car she was passing, which then pulled off the road onto the shoulder to avoid being hit. Edna and the oncoming car had a head-on collision, and both drivers were killed instantly.

"According to the police report, Edna wasn't wearing a seat belt, was probably exceeding the speed limit, and was legally drunk. So, she caused not only her own death, but also that of the driver of the oncoming car."

"Oh, Grandma, Mrs. Johnson wasn't a nice person. How awful that she caused not only her own death, but also that of an innocent driver as well!"

"Yes, Dear. We were pretty shaken up when we got the news from Mr. Johnson. By the way, Jim, how's George doing? I saw you talking to him over the fence a few minutes ago."

"Well, the news is that one of the Casserole Club ladies from our church has found a way into George's heart by way of his stomach."

"What's a Casserole Club lady, Grandpa?"

"Well, when a man's wife dies, the divorced or widowed ladies of our church take it upon themselves to feed the man. Mostly, they bring casserole dishes. One particular Casserole Club lady brought George not only casserole dishes but desserts too. He told me that over this past year, the list has grown from chocolate chip cookies, brownies, and apple pie to also include blueberry muffins, banana nut bread, and cinnamon rolls. It turns out that she is a fabulous cook. Not only that, but she has a wonderful sense of humor, an endearing smile, and is a good listener. He can't say enough about what a wonderful wife she would be. So, they started dating and he fell in love. Last week he bought the biggest engagement diamond he could afford and proposed. She said 'yes.' They will be married this summer and take a honeymoon cruise to Alaska."

"Will they live in his house, Jim?"

"No, he'll sell his house and move into hers. It's bigger and roomier."

"Looks like you'll have new neighbors on both sides of your house, Grandpa. I hope they will turn out to be as nice as the Olsens were."

"We'll just have to wait and see, Laura. We'll just have to wait and see."

Airport Blues

"Have you got your boarding pass?"

"Yes."

"Do you have money to tip your Ace Express van driver?"

"Yes."

"Have you charged your cellphone?"

"Yes, Grandma. Don't worry. I'll be fine."

"And be sure to call me as soon as you get home."

"Don't worry so much, Grandma. I'm a big girl now. I'll be graduating from high school in June."

"I know, Elizabeth, but I remember all too well a trip I took to visit your parents before you were born. We didn't have cellphones then or boarding passes, and we didn't have to go through an airport security checkpoint before we boarded the airplane. We bought our tickets at the airport."

"If you didn't have cellphones, how did you communicate if you needed to call somebody?"

"There were pay phones in various places in the airport. All we had to do if we needed to call someone, was to drop a dime in a slot in the pay phone, wait for the dial tone, and punch in the number of the person we wanted to call. The only problem was you needed to have enough change if the number was long distance. There was an extra charge for that."

"What could you do if you had any kind of a problem?"

"Well, I was just now remembering a problem that I *did* have the time I went to visit your parents. Would you like me to

27

tell you what happened?"

"Yes, please."

It was a clear sunny October day in Sedona. The Ace Express van picked me up at exactly 8:00 a.m. to take me to the Phoenix airport. The driver greeted me with a smile, shook my hand, and said his name was Ray. He was a tall, lean fellow, dressed in Levis, a cowboy shirt, black boots, and a black cowboy hat with a feathered hatband. It was a typical Arizona outfit.

Since I was the only passenger, he asked me to sit up front, and we chatted all the way to the airport. The hour and forty-five minute drive passed quickly. At the airport, we went directly to the Northwest Airlines curbside check-in area. Ray unloaded my two heavy suitcases and carry-on bag. I opened my purse and got out of the van to tip him a few dollars. Then, Ray waved a cheerful goodbye as he drove off.

A young Hispanic fellow, sporting a trim mustache and dressed in a brown luggage-handler uniform, greeted me. He had a dolly with him.

"Sorry, ma'am, but there's no more curbside check-in since the September 11th disaster. Can I help you with your luggage? It looks pretty heavy."

"That would be wonderful," I said. "I'd be very grateful for your help."

He escorted me to the line at the Northwest check-in desk. As he unloaded my bags, I reached in my purse to tip him. I couldn't find my wallet. I searched my large travel purse and unzipped three different compartments. Still no wallet! I rummaged again and again through the rest of my purse. The missing wallet was just *not there*! A look of disbelief must have shown on my face.

"What's the matter?" the luggage-handler asked.

"I can't find my wallet. Not only does it have a lot of money in it, but also my driver's license, my credit cards, and my medical insurance cards. What am I going to do?"

"Well, you can't check in without a photo ID," he said. "Maybe you dropped it at the curb when you opened your purse to tip the driver. Let's go back there and look for it." He reloaded my bags on the dolly and we went back to where Ray had left me.

We searched the street, the curb area, and the sidewalk. Nothing!

I guess I'll have to call Ace Express, I thought, *and have them pick me up and take me home.* Then, I said aloud, "I can't even make a phone call. My coin purse is part of my wallet."

"Don't worry, ma'am. I'll stay with you until we get this problem straightened out," said my companion. "I believe there's a telephone under the Northwest check-in desk. If it's still working, you can use it without charge."

"Thank you," I said. Fortunately, I had the 800 number for Ace Express written on my itinerary. I called and explained what had happened. They said they would send a car for me right away.

Each minute that passed seemed like an hour. I had just about given up hope when I saw a van pull up. Ray was driving. He signaled me with a big smile and his outstretched hand waved an okay sign.

As he got out of the van, I could see my wallet in his hand. I ran toward him and gave this tall, lanky cowboy a tremendous hug as he bent down to hug me back.

"Did you get my message?"

"Yes," he said. "I stopped to get a bite to eat after I left you. I called the office to ask if there were any messages. They told me about your problem and suggested that I look in the van for your wallet. It was on the floor in front of your seat. I came as soon as I could."

"Thank you, thank you so much!" I said over and over.

Walking back to his van, Ray waved goodbye and said, "Have a safe trip and enjoy your family."

It occurred to me afterwards that I should have given him a generous tip. But he was gone in an instant, back to Sedona.

"I'll help you get checked in," said my companion. He had stayed with me for over an hour. With his help, I was able to quickly get back to the check-in desk.

"Don't worry," he said as he looked at the board above the desk. "Your flight has been delayed. You'll make it to your gate on time."

I checked in. Then, I turned to thank my luggage-handler and to tip him for his generosity and time. He was gone. I hadn't even had a chance to say thank you.

Angels come in different attire. This beautiful one wore a brown luggage-handler uniform. I believe that he must have been my guardian angel.

"Do you think that if I have a problem, my guardian angel would rescue me?"

"Yes, Dear, I do."

"So you see, Grandma, you shouldn't worry about me. I'll be fine, and I will definitely call you as soon as I get home."

The Gigolo

It was four-thirty on a hot, humid afternoon in July when I boarded the Spanish freighter, Santa María, in Cartagena, bound for Tenerife in the Canary Islands, Gibraltar, and Barcelona. My French friend, Lulu, was supposed to be boarding with me, but she had broken her nose in a fall and had to cancel her trip aboard the freighter. She would fly to Paris at a later date and I would take the train up to meet her. We would stay at her aunt's house in the Paris suburbs and use it as a base, going from there into the city for sight-seeing. I looked forward to visiting the Eiffel Tower, Notre Dame Cathedral, the Louvre, and other famous Paris landmarks.

We both were students at the University of the Andes in Bogotá, and had met during enrollment. She was born in Colombia, but her parents were from France. Our common language was Spanish, but as soon as we met she asked if we could exchange my English lessons for her French lessons. She liked my American accent. That was the beginning of our friendship.

When classes at the University were winding down to summer vacation time, Lulu asked if I would be interested in going to France with her. We could go by freighter, which was cheaper than flying, and with our student discounts could get our meals and sleeping accommodations included in our ticket. I had never traveled anywhere by sea. It would be a new experience. I never thought I'd be going alone.

When I found my room, my new roommate was already settled in the bottom bunkbed of our small quarters. She introduced herself as "Elena". She was Colombian, probably in her mid-twenties and what you would describe as "petite gamine". Her dyed red hair was cropped short. She wore dark pants and an off-the-shoulders white blouse. She was smoking a cigarillo. After I introduced myself as "Marisa", she told me that she would disembark at Tenerife and meet her husband, "El Tigre", who was a popular Colombian wrestler. I told her that I was a student from Los Andes University and that I was getting off in Gibraltar. She didn't seem to be interested in learning more.

After we got settled in our cabin, we went to the tourist class salon to meet the other passengers. Two American males were drinking beer when we arrived. One introduced himself as "Crash". He told us that became his name after he had crashed his motorcycle so many times in racing competitions. His companion introduced himself as "Bob". Bob appeared to be in his mid-thirties. A third male passenger introduced himself as "Carlos". He was probably in his early twenties. We spoke Spanish. The five of us would be traveling companions for the week we were at sea. The upper deck, reserved for first class passengers and officers, was to be off-limits. We were to eat in separate dining rooms. During our common voyage we would see little of them.

After a day or two, our common get-together place became the tourist bar. The ship's swimming pool was another place to get to know one another as we all worked on our summer tans. Our dining room was a third meeting place, but my appetite vanished at the menu. I was seasick most of the day and the food offered was heavy, greasy, and totally unappetizing.

The bar was where we mostly met up for coffee, Coke, and conversation. When Carlos and Elena were absent we spoke in English. We talked about ourselves and I learned that Crash and Bob were CIA agents, or so they said, who had completed their current tour of duty and were on their way to Barcelona and a vacation in Spain. I suspected that they were lying, but they were fun to talk to.

Almost immediately, Elena started flirting with a lower deck crewman and within a couple of days seldom joined us in the bar after breakfast. She was always asleep when I left our room and we rarely saw her before lunch. She would join us at the pool, but didn't talk much as she worked on her tan.

Crash and Bob traded their coffee for beer almost immediately after breakfast. Soon they were telling jokes and getting us to laugh. Their Spanish was limited, their grammar atrocious, and their American accent obvious. All of this lent an element of hilarity to their attempt at communication. Carlos and Elena were just as much lost with Crash and Bob's Spanish as with their English, but they were good-hearted and covered up their not understanding with hearty laughter.

Carlos was Mexican. He was tall, with black curly hair, and looked terrific in his bikini swimsuit lying by the ship's swimming pool showing off his well-muscled young body. He was the perfect picture of tall, dark, and handsome. My Spanish was quite fluent, so Carlos seemed to be more comfortable talking to me more than to our American companions. He wasn't what you'd call "flirtatious", but he did single me out for conversation. Over the course of a week I got to know him quite well. He liked talking about himself, especially after a couple of beers at the bar. He told me that he'd grown up in a poor neighborhood in Mexico City. He was hungry most of the time, and resorted to petty theft as a "child of the streets". Little by little, in fragments of conversation in the bar and at poolside, he told me his story.

"I was about fourteen or fifteen at the time when I got caught stealing the hubcaps off a parked Mercedes Benz in downtown Mexico City. It was getting dark at the time and I assumed from some boutique labeled bags in the car that the driver was a woman. I pictured her out still shopping or having late afternoon tea in a nearby tea room, so I thought I had plenty of time to get away with my theft. I was wrong. However, I was in luck that she didn't immediately call the police, but instead she admonished me severely. The she told me to get into her car and we headed toward her apartment in an upscale residential district.

As we drove, she asked me about myself, my life on the streets, if I had much schooling, and about my family. I told her as honestly as I could what she wanted to know. I was used to lying, but I felt that she needed to know the truth—that I was the oldest of a large brood of children produced by my mother, and that I didn't know who my father was. My mother had had several lovers, some of whom left her with offspring. She took in laundry to feed us. From an early age I skipped school for the tourist section of Mexico City to beg for a few coins to help my mother. At that time I could read a little, write my name, and not much else. Later, taught by street kids, I learned to steal, nothing big, just what brought in enough to fill up my empty belly. I learned about money and how to risk my freedom to get it and hopefully not get caught.

Then, something quite unexpected happened. As soon as we arrived at her home she asked if I was hungry. Of course I was. I had planned to sell the hubcaps and treat myself to a decent meal. I hadn't had much to eat for several days. I don't remember what she fed me, but I was so hungry I know I must have stuffed myself like it could have been my last meal.

While I was hurriedly shoveling down my dinner, she told me that I was going to take a shower and stay with her that night. In the morning we would go shopping and she would buy me a whole new wardrobe. The clothes I had worn would be thrown in the trash. Then she was going to enroll me in a neighborhood school. I was to be known as her "nephew" whose mother had recently died and that she was now my guardian. My life had just taken a dramatically different path."

Carlos continued his story the next day at the pool with

intermissions to get a beer. I joined him with my usual Coke. It seemed to be the only beverage that quieted my queasy stomach.

Back at the pool, Carlos resumed his story. I listened, fascinated, without interruption.

"My lady, I found out later, had been married to a much older, very wealthy man who had died shortly before we met. She, herself, had come from a poor family and married, not because she loved him, but because she wanted the kind of life he could offer. She taught me what she had learned from her husband concerning good table manners, appropriate talk at social gatherings, and how to dress for any occasion.

For my sixteenth birthday she gave me driving instructions, and, from then on, I was her chauffeur. Our relationship began to change. I became the man of the house. She had always treated me with little gestures of approval and affection, but soon those hugs and kisses lasted longer. I responded in kind, but soon found that I wanted more, needed more. My manhood was awakening. She seemed to recognize this.

By my eighteenth birthday we were sharing the same bed. She taught me everything she knew about love-making and how to please her. She gifted me with the most expensive clothing, my own car, anything I wanted. Then, unexpectedly, she got very sick, and within a short time my lady died. As she had spent most of her wealth on extravagant spending during our years together there was little left except debts and taxes. I was back on the streets. I had no job skills, but I knew how to please a woman. That became my livelihood. In no time at all I was living with another widow. I exchanged her for one with more money, and so it went."

I asked Carlos why he was on this voyage to Spain.

"I was bored with my last lady. I wanted to travel, see

other countries, other vistas. Spanish is my only language of communication, so I decided to start in Spain. I had some money saved, left my patroness and booked this freighter to Barcelona. I have heard that escort services provided by the city's expensive hotels is a good way to meet wealthy women traveling alone. As soon as this boat docks I'll be heading for the nearest up-scale hotel to offer my services as an escort. I have the clothes, the manners, and the know how to charm the ladies. I'll start there. I am sure that eventually I'll find a widow who will keep me in the style I have been accustomed to."

The days passed pretty much with the same routine. Crash and Bob, Carlos and I meeting in the bar after breakfast, then meeting up again poolside. Elena still was not present. She was sleeping off a long night with her lower deck sailors. Later that afternoon, when I returned to my room to change for dinner, she was awake. It was no secret that she spent her nights enjoying herself. Days were for recuperating with long naps. If I awakened her by coming into the room to change clothes, or for any other reason, she got angry. I learned to open the door to our room very quietly and tip-toe around the room so I wouldn't wake her up. Going to bed was no problem. I pretty much had the room to myself until after midnight. Elena was no Cinderella. By now she was enjoying, or so she told me, several young Spanish Prince Charming crew members as lovers. She had no favorites. Their sexual encounters took place late at night in one of the life boats attached to the main deck. She offered to introduce me to one of the sailors who had seen me poolside in my bathing suit and liked what he saw. I declined.

"What's the matter with you, woman? Don't you like men? Or maybe you already have a lover in that Mexican, Carlos? No?"

I turned and left our room without any further conversation. I had to admit to myself that I was attracted to

Carlos. I didn't know how he felt about me. Our relationship had not gone beyond our being friends. He liked to tell me about himself. I liked being the listener. Besides, Carlos was a gigolo and I couldn't afford him.

The next morning at breakfast Carlos was missing. He didn't appear in the bar for coffee, nor did we see him the rest of the day. He wasn't at dinner either. Crash provided the answer to my question: "Where is Carlos?"

"He's in first class with that German widow who spotted him in his skin-tight skimpy bikini bathing suit at poolside. She must have been watching with her binoculars. I got the story from one of our breakfast waiters. He saw Carlos sneak into her room on the upper deck last night and he hasn't reappeared yet. I suspect he found his new meal ticket."

We didn't see Carlos again in tourist class. Crash's informant said that Carlos had moved into the German widow's suite. They had their meals delivered by room service.

I've often wondered what happened to Carlos. Did he find what he was looking for in a long term relationship with the German widow? Or, if he went on to become an escort in an upscale hotel, did he finally find a woman who could provide the life style he so wanted?

He may have been a gigolo and earned his living making love to rich widows, but he was honest about himself, and a captivating companion. I'll never forget him.

A Perilous Trail

My sister-in-law, Carol, had come up from Los Angeles to our cabin in Lake Arrowhead for a few days. My brother had recently died, and I felt that the fresh mountain air and beautiful scenery would be good for her. Little did I know what was in store for us that day. It was just the two of us at Lake Arrowhead. My husband had opted to stay at our condo in Pasadena so he could do some work at the office. He planned to join us on the weekend.

Carol felt like taking a drive up to Big Bear Lake, which we did. Then, we stopped at a little café for lunch and, on the way back to the cabin, I suggested that we stop and stretch our legs at a nature trail provided by the forest service. I had walked this trail many times with my parents. It was circular and easy, no more than three-quarters of a mile long.

We parked in front of the entrance, and I put my purse under my seat.

Carol said, "I'm taking my purse because I have a lot of money and my cigarettes in it. I'll probably want to smoke as we walk along. You'd better take your purse, too. Someone could break into the car and steal it while we're gone."

Rather than take it with me, I hid my purse further under my seat where it couldn't be seen. We walked up to the entrance, read the information on the bulletin board, and started off to the left. We took our time, stopping to read the plaques that identified the various kinds of pine cones and the trees from which they came. There were even boxes filled with pine cones under some of the trees.

As we walked along, we were soon approached by a very thin, scruffy young man coming from the opposite direction.

His hair was matted, and he had a dirty, scraggly beard. His clothes were filthy and looked like he'd slept in them.

He walked right up to Carol and leaned into her face. "Have you got a cigarette?"

"No!" She backed away from him, clutching her purse to her chest. She told me later that she was afraid that if she had opened her purse to give him a cigarette, he would have snatched it from her. And she didn't want to lose her purse and her money.

The intruder spun around and stomped away, heading back the way he'd come. He rounded a bend in the trail and we lost sight of him.

We continued our walk. A short time later we heard a very frightening sound. "Whack! Whack! Whack!" We walked on to get a closer look. What we saw struck terror in our hearts!

The man was beating a heavy stick against a huge tree trunk, seeming to test the stick's strength. His face was contorted with rage as he yelled out the vilest obscenities directed toward women. From the sounds and sight of the man's fury, we felt sure that Carol and I were to be his targets.

"Marisa, he means to kill us," Carol whispered. "What shall we do? Should we try to fight him together, or should we run like the devil himself is after us back to where we started, and pray that we get to the entrance before he does?"

"We're no match for him, Carol," I said. "He probably wants our money for drugs. He's crazy. We'd better run for it."

We ran as fast as we could, Carol in the lead. Along the way, I silently prayed to my guardian angel to save us from this very dangerous turn of events. But as we approached the entrance to the trail, we could see that the stranger had arrived first. He was sitting on a bench with his club between his knees.

We stopped before he saw us and moved close to the trees and out of his sight.

"What shall we do?" asked Carol. "The trail is surrounded by a tall wire fence, and we can't climb that. The only way out is through the entrance."

"Pray," I said, and we did.

Then a miracle happened. Two forest rangers drove up to the parking lot and walked over to the bulletin board to put up a notice. The young man hung his head and looked away from the rangers. We took that opportunity to walk out and head for our car.

"Afternoon, ladies!" one of the rangers said. "It's a beautiful day for a walk. Hope you enjoyed it!"

We just smiled, waved hello, and quickly got in our car and drove away. Little did the forest ranger know what we had just gone through.

Or perhaps he did know. Could he have been my guardian angel and the second ranger Carol's? Some people may doubt it, but we're convinced that they had come to rescue us just in time!

Fork in the Road

As Elizabeth sat in her comfortable, blue upholstered chair, morning tea in hand, she glanced out the nearby window with a view of the adjoining red sandstone rock gulley and watched her ground squirrel neighbors as they foraged for their breakfast. Their favorite place seemed to be underneath a large mesquite tree which grew on the edge of the gulley on the adjoining empty lot.

Sipping her tea, she watched two young ground squirrels chasing each other in and out of the crevices and gaps in between some larger rocks, as if they were playing tag. In and out, in and out, around and around they raced, finally disappearing under a large gray boulder.

Meanwhile, an older mature male was chewing on a twig he had found underneath the mesquite tree. Something startled him. He dropped the twig and scurried into a crevice between two large red rocks. Then, he ventured out again. This time he chose a stalk of field grass to chew on. Seemingly fearful, and always on the alert for predators, the squirrel, in a constantly agitated motion, moved his head first left, then right, left/right, straight ahead, all the while chewing on the twig he held tightly in his mouth.

Watching her rock squirrel neighbors while she sipped her morning tea had become a ritual for Elizabeth since she had lost her husband to a fatal heart attack the previous Thanksgiving. Now, a year later, she was alone. There was no longer a reason to cook a turkey with stuffing, bake a pumpkin pie, or set a Thanksgiving-themed table for two. The sensible thing to do if she wanted a traditional Thanksgiving meal was to go out to dinner. So, Elizabeth had made a reservation at a nearby restaurant called Fork in the Road. She had hoped for a dinner invitation from neighbor friends, but they had opted to visit their children in California.

"Why in the world am I going out to Thanksgiving dinner alone?" she asked herself. *"I don't want to go! It was a stupid thing to do, to make a reservation for one at the Fork in the Road. I'll have to get dressed up, sit by myself, and watch couples and families enjoying being together for the holiday."*

She sighed, and then made up her mind to cancel her reservation.

Elizabeth finished her tea, got up from her chair and went to her kitchen desk. She looked up the telephone number of Fork in the Road and called the restaurant. Before the phone was answered, she hung up.

"Well, what's done is done. I'm not going to change it. Besides, John would want me to go out tonight and enjoy a turkey dinner for both of us."

The next thing to do was to decide what to wear to the restaurant. Elizabeth went through her dress-up clothes and took out everything black in her closet to possibly wear to dinner that evening. Black seemed appropriate for her widowed status. But she eliminated the black dress and matching jacket she had worn to John's funeral, as well as the black wool pants, white silk top, and black cashmere three-quarter sweater coat she had worn to the evening memorial party given by John's law firm. The clothes held too many painful memories, so back in the closet they went. One day she would donate them to charity. Back in the closet also went the subtle black-and-white tweed suit and the black-and-white patterned sweater she often wore with her black wool pants.

Out came a navy blue dress, a medium blue pair of pants with matching jacket, several white sleeveless tops, and a beige lightweight pant suit. When she laid them on the bed, she knew hey wouldn't work. So back in the closet they also went.

"Well," she said to herself, "I guess it's time to go shopping or some happier clothes."

Elizabeth finally decided upon black wool pants, a pretty tan silk top, and a leopard-patterned wool cardigan sweater in soft shades of tan, beige, off-white, and black. The sweater pattern was subtle, quite pretty, and feminine. She left the chosen clothes on her bed and opened her jewelry box to find a complement to her dinner clothes.

John had gifted Elizabeth with jewelry for each of her birthdays, their anniversaries, and their Christmases together. Choosing what jewelry to wear this evening came more easily than choosing which clothes to wear to dinner. She chose a thick gold neck chain that John had given her on their tenth anniversary and the gold, wedding-knot earrings he gave her on their last anniversary. She paired them with a simple diamond-studded bracelet inherited from her grandmother. She would wear no rings, not even her wedding band. It was time to take it off and place it in the gray velvet ring box it had come in and put it into the closet wall safe. After a year of mourning, it was time to acknowledge that her legal status was "widow," a solitary female.

It was a quarter to six--plenty of time to drive the short distance to Fork in the Road, park, and make her six o'clock dinner reservation. A last look in the mirror and she was ready to leave. She checked to see if her purse held the small flashlight she might need to read the menu if the table she had reserved held only a candle for light in a dimly lit dining room. Hopefully, tonight the restaurant would be well-lighted, and she would have no need for her purse flashlight.

The parking lot was almost full, but Elizabeth found a spot near the restaurant entrance. She checked in. Almost immediately she was ushered to a table with two place settings in a quiet corner facing the restaurant entrance.

"Shall I remove the second place setting, Madam?" the waiter asked.

"No," she said. "My friend said that he might be late." *Why in the* world *would I say that?* Elizabeth asked herself.

As she glanced at the menu, she saw that the fixed price dinner offered a glass of wine as part of the meal. So Elizabeth ordered a glass of house Chardonnay to sip as she took her time deciding what to order.

When the waiter returned with her wine, Elizabeth still wasn't ready to order. Somehow the traditional turkey dinner offering didn't appeal to her. She asked for more time to decide.

"I'll return later for your order, Madam. Take your time."

"Thank you. I thought I'd order the Thanksgiving special, but somehow it isn't as interesting a choice as I thought it would be. What else would you recommend?"

"As the first course, I'd recommend our popular butternut bisque soup, followed by the turkey roulade--unless you'd rather have something else, perhaps a dinner salad and a small steak."

"Let me think about it a minute or two. Perhaps my friend is held up in traffic. I'd like to wait a little longer before ordering."

"Yes, Madam. I'll check in with you in a few minutes."

Elizabeth had felt so uncomfortable dining without John that she made up the imagined male friend to share her table. No turning back now. The place setting would remain.

When the waiter returned, Elizabeth said, "I don't know when, or even if, my friend will arrive. His mother is in the hospital and quite sick. He may have had to go there instead of joining me here. Please bring me the butternut bisque soup and another glass of Chardonnay."

"As you wish, Madam. I hope your friend comes soon. I'll leave the place setting."

The butternut bisque was good, but Elizabeth had no appetite for it, or for the turkey roulade, which she had ended up choosing as the entrée. She ate less than half of her order. Then, she pushed her plate to the side as a signal that she had finished.

The waiter came and cleared away Elizabeth's dinner dishes.

"Would you like some dessert now, Madam, or perhaps another glass of wine?"

"No, thank you. Perhaps coffee. Yes, bring me a decaf coffee, please, and you can bring me the check."

"Yes, Madam. It's a pity your friend didn't arrive. I'm so sorry that you had to eat dinner alone on Thanksgiving."

The waiter left and Elizabeth took her time drinking her coffee.

"It was such a mistake to make this reservation. I wish I hadn't done it, and then to lie about a male friend coming. Well, it's not going to happen again."

While she was feeling sorry for herself, a well-dressed, attractive middle-aged man approached her table.

"Excuse me. I see that you are at a table for two. Are you expecting someone?"

"No. I'm alone."

"Well, I didn't make a reservation. So when I arrived, there wasn't a table available. Would it be alright if I shared your table?"

"Yes, of course. It's Thanksgiving Day, and I would welcome your company."

"My name is Ed."

"I'm Elizabeth."

"I lost my wife a few months ago and couldn't bear to heat up a frozen turkey dinner and eat alone on Thanksgiving Day. So, I took a chance on getting a table at Fork in the Road.

"I lost my husband a year ago today and felt the same way."

"So, we have something in common, Elizabeth."

"Yes, it seems so, Ed."

The waiter interrupted their conversation with Elizabeth's check and saw that she had a table mate. He smiled broadly and said, "I'm so glad to see your friend finally came, Madam. I'll bring him a menu right away."

"Oh, waiter, please hold my check. I changed my mind about the dessert. I'll have the pumpkin pie with extra whipped cream."

Getting Naked

"Dr. McFarland, I'm here because I'm sexually attracted to a man I know as a friend. I've known him for some time, but now when we hug upon greeting one another, I want the hugs to last longer. So far, we are what you might call 'platonic, intellectual' friends. That seems to be the kind of man I gravitate to for companionship. If our friendship were to lead to sex, I fear standing naked in front of him, exposing all the scars and disfigurement of my two mastectomies and all the reconstructive surgeries that followed. My instincts tell me that he is also physically attracted to me, but I'm scared. I want to run away rather than face my fear and allow him into my life as a lover."

"Mary, you came to me when your husband died and you were in deep grief. We did a lot of healing work. Now, we must address the issue of whether you can open up your heart enough to love again and to allow your lover to see you naked with all your emotional and physical scars."

"I don't know. That's why I'm here. I feel that if my potential lover sees me naked, all sexual desire he might have had will vanish in an instant. Maybe that's why I've closed my heart to love again. But now I truly want to be with this man physically as well as mentally and intellectually. I want to love and be loved again."

"Dr. McFarland, as you know, I've been a widow for nine years now. In that time, no man has even asked me out for a cup of coffee, let alone a movie, a concert, or dinner. Oh, I've met many men in writing classes, Yavapai Ollie classes, film festivals, chamber music recitals, jazz concerts, and other social outings, but we never get beyond talking."

"Mary, tell me about your special friend. Is he single or married?"

"He's a widower. His wife died some years ago of cancer. I draw the line at married men. I've been there and done that before I was married. Being the 'other woman' is something I never want to experience again. My lover was Catholic, and divorce was out of the question. We were together for two years. Our relationship was primarily sexual. I couldn't call him except at his office, which annoyed his secretary who I had to speak to before she transferred me to him. Sometimes he'd leave me a message that he'd call me back. On occasion, we would go away for a weekend to Palm Springs or some quiet hideaway. Otherwise, we'd meet in my apartment. I began to see less and less of him. I was miserable with no hope for more than a clandestine relationship with a man I thought I loved. Finally, I broke off the affair."

"Mary, let's get back to your special friend. Tell me about him."

"Well, he is college-educated, well-read, loves to travel and explore other cultures, enjoys music, attends both the chamber music and jazz concerts, plays golf, enjoys hiking, and likes dogs—he has a golden retriever."

"I'm more interested in knowing what he is like socially. Is he friendly and outgoing? Does he have a sense of humor and laugh heartily when appropriate?"

"I can answer all of the questions in the affirmative. He has a great sense of humor and I love to hear him laugh. It's infectious."

"We'll get back to your friend later, but now I want to know about your husband and how he reacted to your first mastectomy. Was he supportive?"

"No, he was definitely not supportive. He never hugged

ne again after the surgery because he said that he didn't want
to hurt me. I know that he was withdrawing because he felt he
was going to lose me, that I would die. My first surgery was a
radical mastectomy. Not much was left except skin over bones.
My second mastectomy was less radical. After I healed, I got
silicone implants. They had to be removed when one of them
leaked into my body. They were replaced by salt-water implants.
One of them also leaked, and a third set was implanted. During
those years of surgery, my husband withdrew more and more.
I believed I was losing him. Something had to change for the
better.

"We bought a cabin in Lake Arrowhead, California, and
spent most weekends and vacations there--hiking, swimming
in the lake, and playing cards and board games in the evenings.
Our marriage was healing. I felt we were a couple again. My
husband retired from his L.A. law practice, and we moved to
Sedona. He loved playing golf and joined the local golf club. I
took writing classes. Life was good. Then, he had a major heart
attack, and I lost him. I felt that I'd never open up my heart to
love again."

"And now how do you feel after nine years of being a
widow?"

"I'm ready to love again, but afraid my disfigurement will
interfere with any man being sexually attracted to me if he sees
me naked. Without natural breasts, without nipples, I feel I'm
not a whole woman. That part of me that gave so much pleasure
to my husband is gone."

"Mary, when the man you are attracted to comes to
know you as the whole woman you still are and falls in love
with you, he won't see you as a disfigured female. You are
a loving, compassionate, generous woman who has a lot to
give to a new love in your life. I want you to visualize that
you invite your special friend out for a cup of coffee. You talk

51

a lot, as you usually do, about your mutual interests. Then you spontaneously invite him to your house for dinner, not for seduction, but to get to know one another better. It turns out that you are both ready for lovemaking. After dinner, he embraces you from behind and kisses your neck while you are putting the dirty dishes in the dishwasher. You turn around and embrace him. Your lips meet his…. You finish the story. I want you to write down what you visualized happening next. Bring your visualization to me next week."

A week later at Dr. McFarland's office:

"Well, Mary, did you write down your visualization?"

"I did better than that. I actually *did* invite my friend out for a cup of coffee. We did talk, as usual, for a long time. Then, I spontaneously invited him to my house for dinner. I thought I was prepared that we might end up in bed, but all the old fears of being rejected came up. I silently hoped that he would say that he had another engagement or offer some other excuse to not accept my invitation."

"But he *did*, right?"

"Yes, Dr. McFarland. He did accept. I cooked up a dinner that my husband always seemed to enjoy—beef stew. I made biscuits ahead of time so I could just pop them in the oven to warm up when dinner was ready. Before my friend arrived, I opened a bottle of a five-year-old pinot noir. He had told me in previous conversations that he enjoyed a good red wine with his dinner, and that pinot noir was one of his favorites. He was very knowledgeable about wines and liked to visit wineries on winetasting trips from time to time."

"And then, what happened after dinner?"

"After dinner, he gave me a big hug and a kiss on the cheek and told me how much he enjoyed my dinner. We went into the living room for coffee and some chocolate chip cookies that I had baked that morning.

"We sat down on the sofa next to each other, and he looked at me as if he were seeing me for the first time. I knew that he liked what he saw. He put his arm around me in an affectionate gesture. I drew close and snuggled up. Then, I panicked."

"And then?"

"I moved away. I couldn't look him in the eye. I put my head down. Then, as I told him my story—the one I told you— I held back the tears wanting to run down my cheeks. He listened without looking at me."

"And?"

"He didn't say anything for what seemed like a long time. I was sure that he would tell me that he was sorry and then leave."

"But he didn't, did he, Mary?"

"No. He took both of my hands in his and said, 'Mary, I love you. I'm sorry that you had to go through so much physical and emotional pain, but your breasts were just a part of your physical body that made you feel feminine. In spite of losing your natural breasts, you are still a whole woman. You are a beautiful, intelligent, and kind woman that I want to embrace, caress, and make love to.' He stood up, pulled me to his chest, put his arms around me, and gave me a lingering kiss. I melted and led him to my bedroom."

"And?"

"Well, Dr. McFarland, we took off our clothes and gazed at each other's naked bodies. All I can say is that our lovemaking was beyond my hopes and dreams. I think I can stop looking for a man to invite me out for a cup of coffee!"

The Author

MARISA BONILLA

The Author was educated at UCLA and the University of the Andes in Bogotá, Colombia. She taught English as a Second Language for many years at both the early childhood and university level. She is the author of six children's bilingual / bicultural books, a memoir and a novel. *Pillow Talk* is her ninth publication.

Made in the USA
Middletown, DE
06 January 2023

19090229R00036